A QUICHE TO DIE FOR

THE DARLING DELI SERIES, BOOK 17

PATTI BENNING

SUMMER PRESCOTT BOOKS PUBLISHING

CHAPTER ONE

Moira Darling walked into the deli for the first time in two weeks, and was surprised by how good it felt to be back. Who would have thought ten years ago that she, a single mom, would one day have a job that she loved almost as much as she loved her new husband?

She had met David Morris, a private investigator, a little bit over a year and a half ago. They had been married since summer, but had only recently found the time to go away for their honeymoon. The two weeks they had spent in Europe had been like a dream for the deli owner. The food tour had been David's idea, and she loved him all the more for it. She had come back inspired to create even more new recipes for the deli, and couldn't wait to get started.

"Welcome back, Ms. D!"

Moira stopped in her tracks and looked up. She realized that she had been daydreaming about the honeymoon instead of paying attention to what was going on around her. Hanging over the deli's counter was a banner that read *Welcome Home!* in colorful letters, and two of her employees were waving at her from beneath it.

"Or is it Mrs. D now? Or Mrs. Morris?" Darrin asked. "Either way, welcome back. How was the trip?"

Darrin was the manager of her deli, Darling's DELIcious Delights. He was the person she trusted to handle everything while she was away, and so far had never let her down. Standing next to him was Jenny Goodwin, one of her newer employees. The brunette had been working there since shortly before Moira's wedding, and had quickly proven herself a valuable member of the team.

"Mrs. D is fine for now. We're still discussing whether I should change my name or not, since it's tied in to the store," the deli owner told them. "And the trip was wonderful, thank you for asking."

She and David had been involved in quite a few discussions about whether or not she should take his last name. He thought that it would be better for business if she kept her current last name, Darling. In his opinion, it was more marketable and made sense to keep it, especially if she was ever going to open another store elsewhere. She understood what he meant; her last name was a strong tie to the deli, and she wouldn't want to lose that.

On the other hand, the romantic part of her wanted to take his name. It was the tradition that she was used to, and it felt odd to her to be married to someone without sharing his last name. Luckily, it wasn't a decision that she had to make immediately. She had time to think it over carefully, which was always a good thing to do before making such a big decision.

"You'll have to tell us all about it," Jenny said. "I know Meg is just *dying* to go to Europe. She's going to want to hear everything."

"Well, she'll be glad to hear that I took a lot of pictures," Moira said. "Even better, I came up with tons of new recipes I want to try. I had some of the most amazing food over there."

"Well, you know that we'll be happy to be your taste testers," Darrin said. "Speaking of food, do you want to try the soup and salad combo of the day? It's something Candice came up with."

"Candice? Really?" the deli owner said, surprised. "I

thought she would have been too busy to spend much time over here."

Her daughter, Candice Darling, had opened her own store the year before. It was a small candy shop in the neighboring town of Lake Marion, and was doing much better than anyone had expected ever since they had opened up a website that accepted custom orders. Candice's Candies shipped chocolates and other sweets nationwide for various events and businesses, and the result was a very fast paced, but profitable, business.

Not only was the young woman still learning how to manage her time and balance her business life with her personal life, but she had also gotten engaged to her boyfriend a few months previously. Moira knew firsthand how much time it took to plan a wedding, so she was surprised the young woman had any time to spare whatsoever.

"I guess she had this soup at some restaurant when

she went to out of town and liked it so much that she made her own recipe for it when she got back," Darrin said. "She stopped in a couple days ago and had us all try it. Here, I'll get you a bowl, and you can have lunch while you look over the sales reports from the last two weeks. Everything went well while you were gone. I think you'll be happy to see just how well."

Feeling a bit befuddled, Moira sat at the table nearest the register. Here she was, being served in her own deli. Just two years ago, she had had only two other employees, and one had been her daughter. Now it felt like the deli barely needed her to function. She knew that she should be happy that it ran so smoothly without her — and she was — but it also left her feeling a little bit lost.

The sight of the food that Darrin brought out a few minutes later pushed her worries to the side. She had no idea what sort of soup it was, but it looked good and smelled even better. There was a light side salad with a variety of greens, shredded carrots, and some sort of crushed nut. It took her a moment to identify the dressing.

"Ginger?" she asked, as he set the plate in front of her.

Darrin nodded. "It was tough to find something that would go well with the creamy peanut soup. We decided to go with something simple. The crushed peanuts on top really tie it together. The soup is rich, so the light, fresh salad pairs really well with it."

Moira had never had peanut soup before in her life. She tasted a small spoonful, and was surprised by how flavorful it was. Darrin was right; it was very rich, and she couldn't imagine eating more than a single serving, but it was perfect for the chilly winter weather.

"I love it," she said. "I'll have to remember to tell

Candice thanks. Did she happen to leave the recipe?"

"Yep, it's already in the binder," he said.

"It looks like you've got everything handled," she told him, laughing. "Thanks Darrin, I don't know what the deli would do without you."

She spent the next few minutes going over the sales report for the past two weeks. She was surprised by how well they did. They had made almost twice as many sales as they had been making at this time last year. She knew a lot of that could be put to the fact that they had so many more menu options now — the breakfast quiches had definitely been a hit; there had been a huge sales boost after they expanded their hours — but many of their sales had been made simply through word of mouth. More people knew about the deli now, and it wasn't unusual for people driving through town on their way up north or downstate to make a detour specifically to stop in at the deli.

Even though she was happy to see that the deli's sales hadn't dropped off at all while she had been out of the country with David, it drove home the realization that the deli didn't really need her anymore. That left her with the important question of what she would do now. She had originally decided to open the deli to give her something to do in her spare time, but it had grown to be so much more than that. Sooner or later, she would have to decide whether she wanted to see where all of this could lead and continue expanding the business, or be happy with what she had already done and enjoy her new life as a married woman without the stress that would come with growing the deli.

Just like the matter of her last name, it wasn't a decision that she needed to make immediately. For now, she was going to enjoy her soup, make a cup of coffee, and enjoy the next few hours helping out in the deli. It felt good to be back in Maple Creek.

CHAPTER TWO

"Settle down, you two. Didn't we get this all out of your systems last night?"

Moira pushed the two overly excited dogs back far enough that she could shut the door behind them, then put her purse on an end table and attempted to take off her coat without tripping over one of the pooches. Maverick, the big German shepherd that she had rescued from a dog thief the year before, slipped between her legs and the wall, nearly knocking her over in his excitement. Keeva, the even bigger Irish Wolfhound that had showed up on her doorstep shortly after she had moved into the little stone house, was a bit more polite and kept back further, despite the fact that her tail was whipping back and forth in a blur.

During her honeymoon, her daughter had stayed at her house to watch the dogs. Moira knew that they had been well cared for; Candice was one of the few people that she would entrust the two dogs to, and they both seemed to like her plenty. That hadn't stopped the dogs from being overcome with excitement when she and David had gotten home the night before. She hoped that things would go back to normal soon. If she could have, she would have explained to the dogs that she wasn't going away on a vacation again any time soon, and she would have reassured them that she would be back every evening just like usual, but she knew that they wouldn't understand her.

"All right, all right, let's go get some treats. No, Maverick, don't jump up. There you go, good boy."

She reached up and pulled the bowl on top of the

fridge down. Inside was a handful of homemade dog cookies that Candice had left behind. They looked good enough for her to eat herself. Her daughter had assured her that they were made of human grade ingredients, but with flavors like beef and liver, they probably wouldn't taste too good to a human palate.

She tossed each dog a cookie, and while they were eating she went upstairs to change. It still felt odd to see David's things alongside hers. It had been so long since she'd shared a bedroom with anybody, and she had forgotten how much extra space another person's entire wardrobe could take up.

The decision for the two of them to live together in her house had been an easy one. David's apartment in Lake Marion was far too small for the dogs, and it was double the distance from the deli. She had only bought the house the year before, and neither of them wanted to sell it, even if that would have meant they could have purchased a larger home together. With just the two of them, they didn't need much space, and they both loved the little stone house in the middle of the forest.

Changed and feeling refreshed, Moira went back downstairs in time to see a vehicle pull up the drive-way. She recognized the flashy car that she had helped Candice get for her birthday the year before. A split second later, the dogs came running out of the kitchen straight towards the front door. They had an uncanny ability to recognize the sound of familiar engines, and always seemed to know when she, David, or Candice were pulling up.

Smiling to herself, Moira hurried into the kitchen to preheat the oven, then went to let her daughter in.

"Hey, Mom. Eli says he's sorry that he couldn't make it, but we'll have you over for dinner later this week. Things have been insanely busy lately. Where's David?"

"He's still working," Moira said. "I just got home, and he should be here within the hour. Do you want to help me with dinner?"

"Sure. I can't wait to hear more about your trip."

As the two women began to prepare the ingredients for the family dinner, Keeva and Maverick watched them from behind a baby gate. Outside, it was nearly completely dark, and had begun to snow. By morning, Moira knew that the woods would look like a winter wonderland. Maybe she and David would have time to take a walk with the dogs before work. There was something so magical about a fresh layer of pure, unbroken snow.

"So, does David have a lot of work to catch up on?" Candice asked as she began trimming the fat off the chicken breasts.

"He had a few cases waiting for him," Moira said. "I

know he said he's thinking of hiring an assistant, someone who will be able to do some of the foot work for him."

"That's neat. I doubt he'll have a hard time finding someone. A lot of people think it would be cool to be a private investigator. Is he working on anything interesting right now?"

"He mentioned something about investigating a robbery," the deli owner said. "I don't know who his client is, of course, but they gave him a list of what was stolen and he's going to keep an eye out in the local pawn shops and online for items that match the description. So, if he finds someone selling the stolen items, he'll get the police involved and hope-fully the person that was stolen from will get their stuff back."

"He has such a neat job," Candice said with a sigh. "If I wasn't so busy at the candy shop, I might see if I could be his assistant. I just wouldn't have time, though."

Moira pulled a baking tray out from below the stove and put a layer of foil over it so her daughter could begin laying out the chicken. She watched Candice as she did, a thought occurring to her.

"Are you still happy running the candy shop?" she asked.

"Oh, yeah," Candice said. "Definitely. It's just turning out to be a lot different than what I expected. I thought it would be kind of like the deli is, you know? Slower paced, and you get to know all of your customers. But since most of our sales now are online, it's a lot different. It would almost be easier to only have online sales; on the other hand I really like having the storefront."

"I think it's nice to have a place where your

customers can go to buy candy in person," Moira said. "Besides, I'm sure you get a lot of business from tourists. In the summer, they can go to your store, then when they get home they can order from you."

"That's true," her daughter said. "At least the shop is doing well. I shouldn't be complaining. Is that David?"

Moira looked around to see both dogs standing up and staring down the hall towards the front door. She heard the sound of a car door close, and a moment later both dogs were running to greet the private investigator. The deli owner followed behind them, glancing in the hall mirror to make sure she didn't have any marinara sauce drips on her blouse before opening the door for her husband.

"Hey, you," David said, smiling as he pulled her close for a kiss. "Something smells delicious. What are we having for dinner?"

"Chicken Parmesan with homemade red sauce and some sautéed squash," she told him.

"Sounds wonderful."

He bent down to pat the dogs, then straightened up and shrugged off his coat and hung it up in the hall closet. He turned and raised an eyebrow.

"What?"

Moira had been gazing at him. She looked away, embarrassed. "Nothing... it's just good to see you. It feels weird being back, doesn't it?"

"I know what you mean," he said. "I got used to having you around all the time. My office feels lonely now."

"Bring Maverick with you," she suggested. "He'd love it. He may not be as good for conversation as I am, but he's a great listener and gives world class cuddles."

"I would, but I don't think he'd like the long hours I spend sitting in the car. It's not so bad during the warmer weather when I can have the windows open, but it's a bit miserable during the winter. Of course, with his fur coat, he may be more comfortable than I am."

They both looked down at the German shepherd, who was busily sniffing his master's shoes. He seemed to sense their attention, and after a moment, he looked up at them, his mouth open in a happy pant. David chuckled.

"I'm going to go say hi to Candice and let these two crazy pups out back. Should I start setting the table then?"

"Sure. I still have to finish the sauce, and the chicken breasts just went in the oven, so it will probably be about half an hour before we eat. There's no need to hurry."

"Just let me know how I can help." He brushed by her, then paused and turned back. "I love you, by the way."

"I love you, too," she said, smiling. Their honeymoon may be over, but their lives together were just beginning, and Moira couldn't wait to see what life had in store for them.

CHAPTER THREE

Over the next few days, life settled back into its normal rhythm. At home, she and David and the dogs lived the sedate life of a happy family, and at the deli, she slowly got back into the swing of things and caught up with everything she had missed while she was gone. When Cameron asked for a couple of days off to spend time with a relative out of town, she was more than happy to give it to him. She had been looking for an excuse to pick up some full shifts at the deli, but hadn't wanted to take over a shift that had already been scheduled since most of her employees needed the money. Cameron, who she had learned a few months ago was very well off, probably wouldn't have minded, but she had agreed not to treat him any differently than the others.

Tuesday was her first full day of work after getting back from the honeymoon. She rarely asked her employees to take on twelve-hour days, but she didn't mind doing so herself on occasion. With the breakfast hours beginning at seven in the morning, that meant it was still dark when she left for the day. With a thermos full of coffee to help her wake up, she spent the drive to work going over the recipe for crepes in her head.

Normally, the deli offered mini-quiches for breakfast. Over the past year, they had experimented with a huge variety of flavors and styles, but Moira was ready to try something completely new. It wasn't until she had tried some crepes from a street vendor in Paris that she had come up with the idea for crepes. Like quiches, there was a lot that she could do with crepes, and they were quick enough to make that they could even take custom orders.

Humming happily to herself, Moira unlocked the back door, glancing up into the security camera that David had installed there as she did so. It looked a bit dirty — her to-do list for the week would have to include cleaning all of the cameras and double checking all of the other security equipment. Most of it had been installed over a year ago, and it hadn't been checked since.

She went through the familiar routine of preparing the deli for opening. It didn't take her long to count out the register, put a pot of coffee on, and pull the chairs down. Soon all that was left to do was to flip the sign over and unlock the door. It was time to start cooking.

Half an hour later, she pulled a freshly baked batch of feta cheese and spinach mini quiches out of the oven and set them on the counter next to the bowl of batter for the crepes. She had made a couple of crepes and played around with fillings for her own breakfast, and had a good idea of what she was going to offer the customers. Her favorite had been the blueberry cheesecake crepe, but she wanted to make sure her customers had a couple of options. The crepes would be best freshly made, and it would be easy enough to let her customers build their own.

With the quiches out of the oven and cooling on a rack and the two pots of coffee on the warmer, it was time to go unlock the door and welcome her first customers of the day in. She enjoyed working the breakfast shift; her customers were usually on their way to work or school, so they rarely stayed to chat, but for many of them this was the highlight of their day. A lot of them stopped in every single morning, so over time she got to know them just as well as her regular lunch and dinner customers.

"Welcome to Darling's DELIcious Delights," she said as the first customer, a middle-aged, bald man, walked in. He was a regular, someone who had been coming to the deli since the day it first opened. "Hi, Luis. Our breakfast special today is a plate of freshly made crepes with your choice of filling and a complementary cup of coffee. I suggest the blueberry cheesecake filling, which is made with locally grown blueberries, but all of the options are good. What can I get you?"

"What you just mentioned sounds like it will hit the

spot," he said. "I love this place. You've got something new every day. I never get tired of it."

She smiled. That was exactly what she liked to hear.

Meg came in to help with the afternoon shift just as Moira was putting the finishing touches on the big pot of lobster bisque soup, their soup of the day. She was overwhelmingly pleased with the success of the crepes, but after just one morning, it was evident that she was going to need to begin having two people there for the breakfast shift. Trying to juggle making crepes and managing the register all on her own hadn't been her most brilliant idea.

"Hey, Ms. D," Meg said. "How's it going?"

"We've been pretty busy so far today," Moira told her. "That might change if the weather guy was right, though. We won't have as many customers this evening if it starts to snow."

PATTI BENNING

Sure enough, as the bad weather moved in, fewer and fewer customers came through the door. It was a slow enough day that Moira did something she rarely had a chance to do while she was working these days; she read. Meg pulled a stool up to the counter next to her and flipped though her phone, glancing up occasionally when a strong gust of wind made the windows rattle.

Moira was just about to suggest that they close early for the day when a customer walked in with a blast of icy air at his heels. He wrestled the door shut before approaching the register. His hands were shoved deep into his pockets, and his hood was pulled low over his face, with a ski mask on for good measure. The deli owner didn't blame him; the snowstorm that they had been promised was turning into a full-blown blizzard, and the winter vortex had covered the entire state with frigid temperatures. It was going to be a rough day for anyone who had to be out and about.

28

"Hi," she said. "Welcome to Darling's DELIcious Delights. What can I get you?"

"I don't know." The man came closer to peer at the chalkboard, where the day's specials were written. "How about everything in the cash register?"

In one smooth motion, he pulled a gun out of his pocket and held it steadily at Moira's chest. She froze.

"You, put down the phone," he said, nodding at Meg. "Don't try anything. Keep your hands on top of the counter, where I can see them."

Out of the corner of her eye, the deli owner saw her employee do as she was told.

"And you, open the register. Now."

Moira didn't hesitate. The money wasn't worth getting shot over. She opened the cash register and began pulling bills out. She handed them over, then reached for the change.

"Not that," he said. "You can keep the coins. But give me your ring."

She touched her wedding ring and breathed in sharply. The band of metal meant more to her than all of the cash in the drawer did. It was the symbol of her and David's love, and their promise to be together for the rest of their lives.

"Hurry up," the man snapped.

Reluctantly, Moira slid the ring off her finger and placed it in the man's gloved hand. She had the feeling that if she didn't, the rest of her life might not be very long at all.

"Both of you keep your hands up," the man said as he slid the ring into his pocket and began backing away. "Nice and easy now."

When his back touched the deli's front door, he turned around, shoved it open, and ran outside. In no time at all, he had vanished into the falling snow.

CHAPTER FOUR

As soon as the man had gone, Moira ran across the room to the front door and locked it. Her heart was beating wildly in her chest. They had just been robbed at gunpoint, and the criminal had gotten cleanly away. She didn't care about the money, but the thought of her missing wedding ring made her feel like crying.

Taking a deep shuddering breath, Moira turned to her employee. "Are you all right, Meg?"

"I'm fine, Ms. D," the younger woman said. Her face was pale. "What do we do?"

"I'm going to call the police," the deli owner said. "Can you start turning everything off and cleaning up the kitchen? We're closing early."

Meg nodded. Seeming glad to have something to do, she pushed through the swinging door into the kitchen. Alone in the main room, Moira collapsed onto a stool and rested her head in her hands. That had been one of the most terrifying experiences in her life, and that was saying something. There had been no warning whatsoever; the day had gone from perfectly normal to deadly in the blink of an eye.

After taking a moment to gather her nerves, the deli owner pulled out her phone and dialed the local police station. Once she had told her story to the dispatcher, she hung up and left David a voicemail, doing her best to reassure him that there was no need to worry. She and Meg were both all right, and the robber was long gone.

After that, there was nothing to do but wait.

Normally the Maple Creek police had a quick response time, but she knew that it would probably take them a little bit longer than usual to get there thanks to the bad weather and dangerous roads. It was frustrating to know that every minute she waited meant that the guy who had held her at gun point was getting further and further away.

"Ms. D?"

Moira turned to see Meg standing in the kitchen doorway.

"What is it?"

"I was thinking — didn't the cameras catch that guy?"

"The cameras," Moira said, shaking her head in

amazement. "I can't believe I didn't think of that myself."

The crook had been wearing a ski mask, but still, video footage of him would be useful for the police. A good recording would give them the man's height, an estimate of his weight, and might even catch something, such as a scar or injury, that could help identify him. Going through the footage would at least give her something to do while she was waiting.

The deli owner pulled the stool up to the counter and sat down with her phone. She could access the cameras from an app that David had installed, and did so now. The camera footage was stored for a week at a time, before being erased automatically to make room for new footage. She could also watch a live feed, which was what she clicked on now.

"What the... what's going on?" she muttered. The live feed was completely black, but she wasn't getting any error messages. She wasn't the best with technology, and had no idea how to figure out what was going on. Was the internet down? Or maybe the cameras were dead. It had been a while since she had checked them, but somehow she couldn't imagine that they had all gone down at once.

Moira peered up at the camera over the register and was surprised to see that it looked dirty, just like the one by the back door had that morning. Frowning, she pulled the stool over to it and climbed up. Someone had sprayed black paint over the lens. What she had thought was dirt, was really just flecks of paint that had misted over the front of the camera's casing.

A *whoop-whoop* from outside caught her attention, and she climbed down off the stool just as someone knocked on the deli's door. She could see the red and blue flashing lights of a police car through the snow. The deli owner hurried over to unlock the door and let Detective Jefferson in.

"It's been a while since I've answered a call here," he said. "It's nice to see you again, though of course the circumstances could be better. Is everyone okay? No injuries?"

"We're fine," Moira told him. "It was just me and Meg here, thank goodness. He had a gun, but it didn't go off."

"Can I have a description of the person?" he asked. "I've got a couple of officers in a cruiser outside, and they're going to drive around and see what they can find. Visibility isn't great, but it's worth a shot."

"He was about my height, bulky, and was wearing a dark green jacket with a hood and a ski mask. He had on leather gloves. Driving gloves, not work gloves."

The detective spoke into his radio, replaying the

information to his men. "What did he take?" he asked when he had finished.

"Some money from the cash register. Probably about two-hundred and fifty dollars. And my wedding ring."

He looked up from his notepad and winced. "I'm sorry. We'll do everything we can to catch this person and get you your money and ring back. Did he take anything else?"

"No," the deli owner said. "But there is something... all of the security cameras have been blacked out."

Jefferson raised an eyebrow. "Now that's interesting. That means the robbery here wasn't random. It was planned."

"But why would someone want to rob the deli?" she

asked. "Two hundred and fifty dollars can't be worth the risk of going to prison. We never keep much cash in the drawer, and we don't have a safe. He can't have expected to get much."

The detective tapped his pen on his lips, thinking. "How much is your wedding ring worth, Ms. Darling?"

She told him, feeling the empty spot on her finger with her thumb as she did so. She had just gotten used to wearing the darn thing, but it already felt like a part of her was missing.

"It might be a long shot," said the detective, "but there's a possibility that's what he was after. Have you told anyone else how much it was worth, or posted pictures on social media?"

"Well, our wedding pictures are online," Moira said. "Candice is the only one, other than David, who knows its worth. She wouldn't have anything to do with this, though."

"No, no, I know she wouldn't," he assured her. "But it's possible that she told someone else, someone who wouldn't have any qualms about breaking the law to get something that's worth a few thousand dollars. This isn't the first case we've had where expensive items have been taken during a robbery. There was a similar crime in Lake Marion a couple of weeks back, and the perp was never caught."

"Do you think it could be the same guy?" she asked.

"There's no way of knowing for sure yet," he said. "Now, I'd like to take a look at the cameras and see your security footage. If we can figure out who blacked out the cameras, then maybe we'll be able to figure out the robber's identity. You and Meg just sit tight. I'll want to talk to her before she goes home; just send her out when she's ready."

"I hope you catch him soon," Moira said. "It's bad enough that he stole my wedding ring, but I'm afraid he might really hurt someone if he keeps doing this. If he points that gun at enough people, sooner or later, he's going to pull the trigger."

CHAPTER FIVE

"Here you go. Coffee, cream, and half a packet of hot chocolate; just how you like it."

Moira took the mug from David and held it in her hands. Sugar and caffeine; just what she needed.

"Thanks," she said. "You're wonderful."

"So are you." He sat down next to her and put an arm around her. "You handled the robbery perfectly. A lot of people would have panicked."

"I don't feel like I did anything right. He got away. When it was happening, I was too scared to do anything, but now I feel like I should have tried to stop him. He was probably the same guy who was involved with the case you're working on right now. He's already robbed two places; I'm sure he'll strike again."

"You definitely should *not* have tried to stop him," David said, facing her. "That's how people get shot. Better to let him take the money. Your life is so much more important."

"But he got my wedding ring, too," she said. "I hate that he took it."

"You can always get a new ring," he said. "But I can't get a new you."

She sipped her coffee, touched by what he was saying, but still struggling under a feeling of anger and helplessness. She had never liked being a victim, and she hated the thought that she had just done nothing when faced with a thief. Rationally, she knew that David was right. An unarmed middle-aged woman would have no chance against a man with a gun.

"There's no rush, but when you're ready, can you go over it with me again? I want to know everything — like you said, this man is more likely than not connected to my case. If I can track him down, I'd be able to get your wedding ring back, and solve the case for my client. It's always nice to kill two birds with one stone."

"I don't know if you should try to find him, David," Moira said. "He looked very willing to use that gun."

"I've helped find murderers before," he reminded her gently. "I'll be careful."

"I just don't want anything to happen to you. I know it's your job."

"Hey, speaking of being careful, I don't want you to get involved with any of this, okay?"

The deli owner frowned, hurt. "But I've helped with cases before. And since I've seen him in person, I might be able to help you recognize him."

"That's exactly why it would be dangerous for you to help. He knows you've seen him. If he sees you poking around, he might decide to tie up loose ends."

Moira sighed, but her husband's logic made too much sense for her to argue with it just then. She was tired, and wanted to put the entire incident behind her for the night. Stolen wedding ring aside, she and Meg had gotten off lucky. If things had gone differently, one or both of them might not have been able to go home in one piece afterward.

"I'm going to go make myself a cup of coffee. Do you want to watch something together before dinner? I think one of the shows we like has a couple of new episodes that we missed during our honeymoon," David said, somehow sensing that she was ready to think about something else.

"That sounds perfect," she said. "Coffee and television with my husband, then a nice family dinner. I'm a lucky woman."

***

Word had gotten around quickly. The next day, the deli was busier than usual despite the snowy roads. David had taken the morning off of work to replace the security cameras. Detective Jefferson was still reviewing the footage in an attempt to figure out who had blacked out the old cameras. Moira hadn't received any news from him yet, and knew that she probably wouldn't for a while. Police work rarely seemed to go as smoothly as she used to think it did, and this case wasn't exactly clear cut to begin with.

"You're all set," David said after he finished installing the last camera. "They're the same model as your old ones, so they should work the same. It's a pity about the other set. I'll try to see if there's any way to clean the paint off without wrecking the lens. We could use them around our house and property."

"I've been thinking it would be neat to have a video camera inside so we can see what the dogs are doing while we're gone."

"I was thinking more for security purposes, but that works, too." He grinned at her, then brushed a quick kiss across her lips. "I've got to run. Want me to pick up something for dinner on the way home?"

"I should be back in time to make something," she said. "Have a nice day."

Moira took her place at the register and began taking orders and answering questions. Ringing each customer up took longer than usual, as most of them wanted to chat about the robbery. Their reactions ranged from touching concern, to blatant curiosity. It was nothing that she wasn't used to; the deli had been the scene of mysterious deaths before, and at least this time, no one had been killed. Still, she was glad when a familiar face walked in.

"I heard all about it," Denise Donovan said. The tall redhead was one of Moira's best friends, and a fellow restaurateur. "An armed robbery in Maple Creek... it's the sort of thing that you never imagine could happen to someone you know. Here, I brought you this. I thought you could use some help relaxing."

Her friend heaved a large gift basket that held wine,

chocolate, candles, and a selection of bath bombs onto the counter.

"Thanks," Moira said with admiration. "You didn't have to do anything. I appreciate it, though."

"No problem. This probably wasn't what you wanted to deal with the week that you got back from your honeymoon. What does David think of all this, anyway?"

"He's upset, as you can imagine. He already replaced the security cameras, and he's going to do what he can to track the guy down. If my ring is sold in any pawn shop in the area, he'll hear about it."

"I hope the guy gets caught soon," Denise said. "You don't think he'll come back, do you?"

"I doubt it," Moira said. "David and I think that he

was probably concerned with getting the ring, and less so with the cash. We never keep much in the register. He got just over two-hundred and fifty dollars — that's not exactly worth risking a felony for."

"Hopefully he doesn't hit anywhere else. Between the two of us, we know most of the small shop owners in town."

"I hope so, too. Maybe after hearing about the deli, and what happened in Lake Marion, people will be more cautious and prepared for something like this to happen."

"I'm sure the police or David will be able to track him down eventually. Until then, I told everyone at the Grill to be on high alert. Speaking of, I should be getting back. We can talk more later; I still have to hear about your trip."

Moira waved goodbye to her friend as she left, then glanced at the clock. It was past noon, and she still hadn't heard anything from David or the police. She knew that she was probably just being impatient, but *some* sort of update would be nice. What in the world were they doing?

CHAPTER SIX

David started the video over for the third time. He had the feeling that this was a dead end, but it was the only lead that he had to go on at the moment. Whoever had robbed the deli and stolen his wife's wedding ring — her felt a prickle of anger whenever he thought of it — had known what they were doing. He had investigated a few robberies in his time as a private investigator, and few of the perpetrators had been as cautious as this guy had been. He had taken no chances in being recognized; with the cameras blacked out, the ski mask, and the leather gloves, he had been careful to leave nothing behind that could identify him.

When Moira had told him about the cameras being

spray painted, David had been worried that it might be too late to catch the act on video. The footage was only stored for a week unless Moira manually saved it, and since she had been gone for two weeks, it had been at least that long since she had checked the cameras. The man could have blacked them out at any time; there was no telling how long he had been planning this for.

They had gotten lucky, at least at first. The past week's footage covered the event, but it wasn't as helpful as he had hoped. The footage showed a young man — a teenager, really — wait until Meg left the register to get something out of the kitchen. In a flash the boy, who had been sitting at a table eating a sandwich, ran behind the counter and sprayed over the lens there. On his way out, he hit the one by the front door, and a few minutes later he sprayed the camera at the side entrance of the deli.

The youth didn't match the description Moira had given him in the slightest. Was it possible that the stress of the event had distorted her perception of the robber? He supposed it was, but his wife had always been a clear thinker, even in situations where her life was in danger. He couldn't imagine her mistaking this gangly boy for a large, bulky man.

It was possible that the blacked-out cameras weren't connected to the robbery, but that theory didn't sit well with him. It would be too much of a coincidence. The boy likely worked for the man, or was possibly even related to him. As far as David was concerned, using a teenager to aid in breaking the law was about as low as a criminal could get. He had a couple of other cases that he was supposed to be working on, but catching this robber was now at the top of his priority list.

The video footage wasn't as helpful as he had hoped, but it did give him a straw to grasp at. If he could track down the kid, that would be something. Jefferson, he was sure, had already seen the footage. He was no stranger to working hand in hand with the police. This would be another case where a joint investigation might be helpful. Feeling better now that he knew where to start, David grabbed his jacket, shut down his computer, and headed out the door.

"I was wondering when you'd show up. We don't have anything to share with you yet —"

"I found the kid," David said. He was sitting in Detective Jefferson's office, still wearing his coat. He wasn't planning on being there long.

"Really?" the detective raised his eyebrows. "How did you manage that so quickly?"

"My sister's got a friend whose kid is in the Maple Creek high school. We showed her a frame of the video and asked her if she knew who he was. She gave us a name."

"I'm impressed. I looked through last year's year-book myself and didn't find him."

"He moved here this year," David said. "That was my first thought, too."

"What's his name?"

"Darwin Henley."

The detective wrote it down. "Thanks, David. I'll go talk to him later today. With any luck, this could be the lead that breaks the case."

The private investigator had the feeling he was being dismissed. He liked Jefferson, but sometimes getting information out of him was like pulling teeth.

"Will you let me know what you get out of him?" he asked. "This is my wife's safety we're talking about. I want to be kept in the loop."

"I'll tell you what I can," Jefferson said. "If we get a name, it's yours."

I'd feel grateful, but I know the only reason he's offering to give me that much is because he knows I'm good at tracking people down when they don't want to be found, David thought. He knew he had done the right thing by giving the police the name of the kid who had blacked out the cameras at the deli, but that didn't mean he was going to completely turn the case over to them.

"Right. Thanks," he said, getting up. "I'll be in touch."

Jefferson looked surprised at how abruptly he had ended the conversation, but didn't remark on it. They had been working together for years. The private investigator was sure that the detective knew where he was going now, but it was clear that he wasn't going to do anything to stand in his way.

Out in the parking lot, David checked his watch. It was just after two in the afternoon. If he was quick, he should have time to get to the high school before the final bell rang. With any luck, Darwin Henley would be willing to talk.

CHAPTER SEVEN

Moira was getting frustrated. There didn't seem to be any progress on the case. She missed her wedding ring, and she hated living with the fear that the robber might strike again. She knew most of the shop owners on Main Street, and couldn't stand the thought of any of them being the victim of an armed robbery.

The night before, David had barely made it home in time for dinner. He had been working all day, but when she asked him for updates, he clammed up. She knew that he was afraid she would try to take matters into her own hands — which was fair; she had made some poor choices in the past — but it still rankled to be kept out of the loop. She doubted

Detective Jefferson would be any more willing to share with her. She considered him to be somewhere between an acquaintance and a friend, but even their friendship wouldn't be enough to make him risk getting into trouble for sharing information with her.

She was stuck with trying to read between the lines in the local newspaper, and scouring the internet for any sign of someone trying to sell her wedding ring. David promised her he had a lead, but he wouldn't say anything more. Every time her phone rang, she hoped that it was David or someone from the police station calling to tell her that the man had been caught.

It wasn't until she got to the deli and began losing herself in work that she started to feel better. It was easy to let anxiety take over when she was home alone with only the dogs for company, and had nothing to take her mind off the past few days. Being busy cooking and chatting with the customers and her employees was good for her. Allison, the employee that had been with her the longest other than Darrin, was back from a skiing trip she had taken, and she was horrified to hear about the robbery.

"I didn't have any phone service up where I was," she said as she washed dishes. "When I came back down yesterday, my phone started to blow up. I couldn't believe it — I thought Candice was playing a trick or something at first. I'm glad everyone's all right."

"Me, too," Moira said. "It was frightening while it happened, but now I'm mostly just angry. That guy had no right to take what he did, and he deserves every second of the jail time he gets when he's caught."

If *he gets caught*, she thought to herself. The longer it took, the more she was beginning to worry that he was going to get away with the crime.

An hour later, Moira was in the kitchen preparing more thin slices of beef for the sandwich of the day — French dip with sautéed mushrooms and a home-made sauce — when she heard the wail of sirens from outside. At first, she didn't pay them much attention, but as they got closer and closer, she began to get concerned. Had there been some sort of accident on Main Street?

She left the kitchen in time to see a parade of police cars and ambulances rush by in front of the window. Both Allison and the customer she was ringing up were watching in amazement.

"I wonder what happened?" the customer, a very pregnant woman, said.

"I don't know. Whatever it was, it must be bad," Moira said.

She went back into the kitchen as Allison finished

ringing the woman up. Maple Creek was a small town. Every time she saw an ambulance or fire truck go by, she couldn't help but worry that they were going to someone that she knew. At least this time, the sirens had been heading away from Lake Marion, where her daughter lived and worked.

She put the incident out of her head quickly enough as she went back to slicing the beef. The French dip was proving to be a hugely popular sandwich, and the orders just kept coming in. It wasn't until she and Allison decided to switch places so she could catch a break from working in the hot kitchen that she began to hear rumors of what had happened.

"I was going to get pizza for the kids, but I just had to stop here instead," one woman said. "I thought your store might have been the one that was hit."

"What do you mean?" Moira asked, confused.

"Didn't you hear? Someone got shot during a robbery. My husband called me from work to tell me about it. He said it was one of the shops on the south side of town. I remembered hearing about what happened to you earlier this week, and I was concerned that the person decided to come back and finish the job."

"It wasn't us, thank goodness," the deli owner said. "Thanks for coming to make sure we were okay. I haven't heard anything about what happened yet."

After packing the three sandwiches in a to-go bag for the woman, she rang her up and sent her on her way. Her anxiety had come back full force; it was as if her worst fears had been realized. The robber had struck again, and this time had hurt someone.

Switching places with her employee again, Moira retreated to the privacy of the kitchen and pulled up the local news site on her phone. There was an article about the shooting, posted only a few minutes ago. Only a few lines had been written to go along with the photo of police cars and ambulances sitting in front of the building in question. The deli owner's heart sank as she read it.

A fatal shooting occurred during an armed robbery today at EZ Wheels, a local auto shop. The victim was Edna Jamison, the shop's proprietor. There is no information on the suspect yet.

Taking a deep breath, Moira put her phone down and stared blankly at the wall. She had known Edna. She had *liked* Edna. The woman had been tough, independent, and was a very skilled mechanic. Yet her life had been cut short because of one man's bad decision. A bitter taste filled her mouth. No matter what David said, she was going to do her part to help the police catch her friend's killer.

CHAPTER EIGHT

As soon as she got home that evening, Moira went straight to the computer to see if there had been any update. She was disappointed, but not surprised, to see that there hadn't. Hopefully David would know more. He would be home shortly with dinner, though what she was really hungry for was information.

"Let's go outside, you two," she said to Maverick and Keeva. They were as cheerful as always, and the wet kisses and happy bumps from their old noses helped to lighten up her mood. She still felt terrible for Edna, but she didn't feel quite as helpless as she had earlier in the day. Justice would be served. She was confident of that.

Both dogs loved the snow. She watched them romp together in the backyard from the mudroom door until she heard David's car pull up. She hurried across the house to meet him at the front door. He hugged her the moment that he saw her, wrapping one arm around her and holding the bag of Chinese takeout with the other.

"I'm so sorry," he said.

"Me, too. She was a good person," Moira said.

"She was. A lot of people knew her. She helped so many people in town with their cars."

"She was always willing to work with people if they were in a tight spot financially," the deli owner said. "She didn't deserve this."

"People never do," David said with a sigh. "Come on,

let's set the table. I haven't eaten all day. We can talk more over dinner."

Moira poked at her honey walnut shrimp. It was one of her favorite dishes, but she didn't have much in the way of appetite. She couldn't get over how unfair it was. What gave anyone the right to end someone else's life like that? Her anger over her wedding ring being stolen seemed like such a small thing now.

"When I first heard what had happened, I was worried that it was you," David said suddenly. He had noodles twirled around his fork, but was staring at them instead of eating. "All that people seemed to know was that someone in Maple Creek had been shot. I was picking up my phone to call you when Detective Jefferson called. He knew I'd be worried, and clarified what had happened. He's a good man."

"He is," Moira agreed. "Sorry to have worried you. I should have thought to call and let you know I was okay. I didn't even know what had happened until a customer came in and told me."

"It's all right," he said. "I was actually hoping you wouldn't hear about it at work. I knew you would be upset, since you knew her. I should have been there when you heard."

She smiled at him, touched. She was so lucky to have found a man that was not only handsome and kind, but cared about her so deeply. It made what she was going to say next even harder. She took a deep breath.

"I want to be involved."

"Moira —"

"No, listen to me before you say anything. I under- stand where you're coming from. I'm not trained to defend myself, I don't even have a gun, the killer might recognize me... I get it. But I can *help*. Meg and I both saw him. Yes, he was wearing a mask, but I can recognize his body type and his voice. Candice knows the first person he stole from in Lake Marion; maybe together we can compare our descriptions and come up with something to identify him. Lastly, the guy who robbed me seemed pretty prepared, with the cameras and whatnot. That means that he was probably in the deli before to case it. It will take a while, but I can have the employees help, and together we can go over the footage from the days before the cameras were blacked out. I already saved it. Maybe we can catch the guy on video — I might be able to recognize him by the way he walks or his clothes or something. It's worth a shot."

"Wow," David said when she had finished, his eyebrows raised. "You really thought this through. I think your last idea is a good one. I didn't see him, so it wouldn't make much sense for me to go through the footage alone. If you're willing to do it, it would be helpful. Keep an eye out for anyone who looks suspicious or shady. I've got a book on body language you can have. If he came in to case the deli before robbing it, he was probably feeling nervous or guilty."

"I'll get started during work tomorrow," she told him, feeling just a bit triumphant. She had finally convinced him to let her do *something* to help. "What about everything else?"

"Well, I can't stop you from meeting with the other woman. If you do, though, please be careful about it. There's a very good chance that the robber is someone local. If he sees his first two victims getting together, he might start to get worried. He's just going to get more dangerous if we spook him."

"If she agrees to meet with me, I'll make sure it's somewhere private," Moira said. "I want to do more, though. I was thinking of maybe going around to some of the stores near the deli and the auto shop and asking if anyone inside witnessed anything."

David shook his head. "No," he said firmly. "That's a bad idea. I don't want the killer to think you have anything to do with the case. It would be too easy for him to find out that you're going around and asking questions about him. I don't want to risk that."

"But —"

"Moira, please... for me. I couldn't bear it if you were the next victim. This guy has already killed someone. I don't want to give him any reason to even think about you."

The deli owner fell silent, defeated. She didn't need his permission to do any of that, of course, but it would be hard to go directly against her husband's wishes when she knew he just had her best interests at heart. She didn't want to worry him. She could imagine how she would feel if their positions were reversed — or even worse, if Candice was the one that wanted to chase after a killer.

"All right," she sighed. "I'll stick with going over the security footage for now. If there's anything else I can do to help, just let me know."

"I will," he promised. "And thank you. I know you're good at putting the pieces together. It's not that I think that you can't do it — I'm just afraid of what might happen if the killer finds you before you find him."

Moira shivered. She hadn't thought of it that way. Despite how eager she was to help, she definitely didn't want to end up on the wrong side of another gun.

CHAPTER NINE

True to her word, Moira began reviewing the video footage the next day. It was painfully slow going, even though she watched it on fast forward. Meg volunteered to help, so the two of them took turns during the slower parts of the day. It would have been a lot easier if they knew exactly who they were looking for, but all they had to go on was what they remembered of the masked robber, and that didn't give them much. There seemed to be no end to the number of somewhat larger guys around Moira's height on the tape. She was holding out hope that they might get lucky and the guy would be wearing the same green coat that he had worn when he took her wedding ring, but so far they'd had no such luck.

"What about him?" Meg asked. There was a lull in activity, and they were both in the back watching the footage on Moira's tablet, relying on the bell to tell them when someone came in.

"I think he's too tall," Moira said. "The person that robbed us was my height, and I'm pretty short. Look at him compared to Darrin. Darrin's taller than me, and this guy is taller than him."

"You're right," her employee said with a sigh. "Do you think we'll actually be able to identify him like this? For all we know, he could have been in the first few minutes of the first video that we watched."

"I don't know. I hope we'll be able to notice if someone is acting nervous. If a guy comes in and keeps glancing at the cameras, fidgeting, and shifting his weight, he'll probably stand out. Most people don't get nervous just ordering a sandwich."

"That's true," Meg said. "Man, I'm going to feel really bad if he came in while I was working."

"It's not your fault if he did. It's not anyone's fault. None of you could have known what he was planning."

Unless it was an inside job, a little voice in her head said. She hated the thought. She trusted all of her employees, but couldn't help but think of how convenient it was that the man had come for the robbery not only after she got back from her honeymoon, but during one of her shifts, too. Had he been watching the deli, waiting for her return? Or was it just a coincidence that he had gotten the ring? She couldn't imagine someone committing an armed robbery for cash register change, but she supposed it was possible. Perhaps the criminal had been driven by desperation, not greed.

"How about him?" Meg said.

Moira focused her attention on the screen. Frowning, she rewound the video by a few seconds and watched it again. It showed a large man with a head of thinning, black hair come in from outside. He paused just inside the front door and looked around as if confused. After a moment, he shook himself and continued on up to the counter, where he gave his order. Darrin was at the register, and when he went into the kitchen to give the order to whoever was on staff, the man looked directly up at the camera. He shifted his weight to the other leg when Darrin came back, keeping his hands in his pockets until it was time to pay. When he pulled his wallet out, Moira gasped. He was wearing black leather gloves.

"That must be him," she said, feeling excited. "Good eye, Meg. Now we just have to find out who he is."

"I think I sort of recognize him," the other woman said, squinting at the screen. "I wish he'd look up at the camera again."

Moira rewound the video and paused it in the spot where the man stared up into the security camera. Meg bit her lip, then her face brightened.

"I think he's the pawn shop guy. The one just outside of town. I think it's called Up the Creek or something like that," she said.

"Perfect," the deli owner said. "Thanks a ton, Meg. Do you think you can watch the deli for a little bit? I want to drive over and see if it's the right person before the shop closes. I don't want to waste anyone's time if it's not."

"Yeah, it's not that busy. I'll be fine," Meg said. "Good luck."

Moira donned her coat and grabbed her purse off the counter. She couldn't wait to see the look on David's face when she told him she had found out who the killer was.

81

The full name of the pawn shop that Meg had sent her to was Up the Creek — Hidden Treasures for All Your Needs. It was a run-down little place just outside of town. She must have driven by it a hundred times without stopping. It was a wonder that it had managed to stay in business this long. She didn't know exactly how many years it had been there, but from the look of the place, it had been quite a while.

She pulled into a parking spot and went inside, too eager to see if she was right to be nervous. Yes, David had warned her to keep out of the killer's attention, but surely just going onto the store couldn't hurt. Anyone could stop in and shop. It wouldn't be suspicious at all.

The interior of the store was crowded, packed from floor to ceiling with various knick-knacks. She pretended to browse for a moment, then picked up a casserole dish with a floral pattern on the side and approached the counter.

"Excuse me," she said. "How much is this?" She kept her eyes on the man as she spoke. He was definitely the same one from the video. The only question was, was he the man who had robbed her?

"Six dollars," he said, barely glancing at the dish. "Plus a three percent fee if you use a card to pay."

"I'll be paying in cash," she said. She thought it would be best to buy something, otherwise it might seem odd. An idea occurred to her. "Do you have any rings?"

He nodded and led her over to a glass display case. "Let me know if you want to see one."

She bent over and peered at the rings, hoping

against hope to see her wedding band among them. When she didn't, she felt a stab of disappointment, but quickly admonished herself. Of course, he wouldn't have the ring on display already. It would make a lot more sense for him to wait until the panic about the robberies had died down to try selling any of the stolen goods.

"Just the dish," she said, walking back to the register. "Thanks."

As he rang her up, she watched him closely. It was harder than she thought it would be to be sure that he was the man who had pointed a gun at her. He was the right height and about the right size. It was his voice that was the hardest for her to feel certain about. The man who had robbed the deli had a deep voice. This man's voice was slightly higher, but that didn't mean it wasn't him. He could have been trying to disguise his voice during the robbery.

"Four dollars back," he said, counting the ones into her hand. "You're all set."

She left, clutching her new casserole dish as she tried to come to a decision. Was it him? She thought back to the video and those black gloves of his. *It has to be,* she decided. *Now to tell David.* Hopefully by this time tomorrow, the man would be in jail, she would have her wedding ring back, and Edna would have justice.

CHAPTER TEN

"I'm sure you're tired of talking about the robbery," said Martha Washburn. "Tell us about your trip, instead."

Martha, one of Moira's closest friends, and Denise were sitting with the deli owner around a round table in a corner cafe. All three of the women worked a lot, so on the rare occasion they were all free at the same time, they grabbed the opportunity to get lunch or a coffee together.

"I want to hear about it, too," Denise said. "I bet Europe was just beautiful, even in winter."

"It was," Moira agreed. "I don't regret going in January at all. Tickets were much less expensive, and there were fewer other tourists around. Everyone was super nice, too."

"How many different countries did you go to?" Martha asked.

"Well, we took the train to get around, so we went through more countries than we actually stopped in. We stayed over in Germany, Belgium, France, and Italy."

"Which was your favorite country?" her friend asked.

"It's hard to say. I liked the food in France the best. Germany and Belgium had some really beautiful natural scenery though, and I'd love to see Italy in the summer."

"I'm so jealous," Martha said with a sigh. "I'd love to go to Europe sometime in the next couple of years."

"It's nice there," Denise said. "I went to Greece a couple of years ago. Were you sad to leave, or was it good to get back?"

"A little bit of both," Moira admitted. "I miss spending so much time with David. It was nice to be able to just focus on being together."

"I bet it was," Denise said wistfully. "I loved being on my honeymoon when I got married. We went to the Bahamas, and it was like paradise. I wish we could have lived like that forever; no stress, good food, and amazing weather." She laughed dryly. "Maybe my marriage would have lasted if we had never left."

Denise had gotten divorced the year before. Her husband had been having an affair, and hadn't even argued when she had mentioned ending their marriage. Moira knew that she was happy to be out of a bad relationship, but she was sure her friend still missed the man her husband had been when they had first married.

Thoughts of Denise and her ex-husband made Moira think of her and David. They hadn't fought at all on their honeymoon, but had already had two arguments since they had been back. Not only that, but she still hadn't told him that she had broken her promise to him and had gotten physically involved in the investigation. After visiting the pawn shop the evening before to verify that he was indeed the man in the video, she had returned to the deli and had simply told David where to look. He had access to the footage himself, so it was easier than having him come all the way over from Lake Marion, where his office was. Knowing that the truth would only concern him, she hadn't mentioned that she had stopped by the pawn shop first.

Truth be told, she still wasn't certain that he was the right person. She had thought it would be easy to recognize the man who had threatened her with a gun, but it was proving to be harder than she thought. Had he really been as large and deep voiced as she thought, or had her fear made him seem bigger than he really was? Still, the man in the video was a pretty good match. The fact that he looked so shifty when he came into the deli, paired with the black gloves, made her think that it was probably him.

She didn't know if David had checked him out yet. He had promised to call if the police made an arrest, so the fact that her phone remained silent probably meant that if he had been to see the man, he hadn't found anything to tie him to the crime.

"Are you all right?" Martha asked. "You seem distracted."

"I'm fine. Just thinking about the robbery and what happened to Edna," she replied.

"It's horrible," her friend said. "I know someone whose brother worked for her. He was there when it happened."

"Really? Did he see anything that might help catch the guy that did it?" Moira asked.

"He already spoke to the police. I don't think he saw anything different than what you saw — a hooded guy wearing gloves and a mask."

"This guy sounds like he's pretty cautious," Denise said. "That's not a good thing. I don't like smart criminals."

"I wonder why he shot her," the deli owner mused. "He didn't try to hurt me or Meg when he robbed the deli."

"From what I heard, she attacked him with a bat," Martha said. "He shot her when she swung at him."

Denise gave a low whistle. "Wow. Poor woman. I can't blame her for wanting to stop him, but it cost her her life."

"I didn't even think of resisting," Moira admitted. "I just did what he told me and handed over the cash and my ring. I felt bad for not being brave, but at least I'm still here now. It really puts it in perspective."

The three women fell silent for a few moments, each of them lost in thoughts about the recent streak of crimes. Eventually the deli owner sighed and stood up.

"I should get going," she said. "I've got to stop by the deli and go over tomorrow's recipe with Darrin. I'll see you two later."

"See you, Moira."

She waved goodbye to her friends, then dumped her empty coffee cup in the trash can. She stood aside as the café's door opened and nodded at the man who came through.

"Good morning, Ms. Darling," he said.

"Good morning, Luis."

He was one of her regulars, someone who had been coming to the deli almost since the first day it had opened. The familiarity with her customers was one of the things that she loved about Maple Creek. Despite everything that was going on, they really were a community.

In her car, she glanced at her phone one last time before pulling out of the parking lot. Still no call from David. She felt bad about not being completely honest with him about going to see the man at the pawn shop. *I'll tell him tonight*, she resolved. *There shouldn't be secrets between us. If there's one person I can trust completely, it's him.*

Dinner that night was fresh baked trout, roasted potatoes and garlic, and a salad that Moira had thrown together herself. When David came in the door, he remarked on how good it smelled.

"I'm never going to regret marrying a cook," he said with a smile. "Though I'd still love you even if you were the sort of person that burned water whenever you tried to boil it."

"That's good to know," she said, giving him a kiss on the cheek. "You love me for more than my food. I'm sure the food doesn't hurt, though. Do you want to sit down? I set the table."

"Let me take my coat off first," he said, chuckling. "I'll join you in a minute."

They sat down together and dug in. Moira was proud of the meal. She didn't cook fish often, but the trout had turned out great. The potatoes and garlic weren't too shabby either. It was a simple recipe — the redskin potatoes were cubed and tossed with olive oil, salt, and pepper before being baked with cloves of garlic.

"I want to say something," David began after they had been eating for a few minutes. Moira looked up, surprised. She had been just about to say almost exactly the same thing.

"What?"

"I'm sorry for telling you what to do," he said. "You're

my wife, but you're also your own person and I shouldn't be trying to control what you do. You know I want you to be safe, but in the end, it's your choice whether you get involved with things like looking for a murderer. I understand why you want to be involved; it's personal, and you're one of the few people that has actually seen the guy."

"Thank you," she said slowly. This was unexpected, that was for sure. Was he going to let her start helping him with more of his cases? An idea occurred to her. She knew he was still looking for an assistant... what if instead of hiring a stranger, *she* became his assistant? She didn't need to work at the deli as much as she had been; her employees had most of the shifts covered, and most of the time they really didn't need an extra person, especially during the slowest times.

She resolved to think about it later. She wasn't sure what all David had in mind for his assistant to do, and she didn't want to get stuck filing paperwork or something boring like that. Not that she wouldn't be willing to help David with that if he needed it, but what she wanted was something more exciting.

"I've got something I've been wanting to talk about too," she said instead. It was time to come clean about her visit to the pawn shop. No secrets meant no secrets, not even harmless ones. And especially not ones involving potential murderers.

CHAPTER ELEVEN

A day spent shopping with her daughter was an opportunity that Moira didn't think she would ever turn down. It was a Saturday, and Lake Marion, while not exactly bustling, was certainly a busy little town. Candice met her mother at the door with her calico cat, Felix, in her arms. She had gotten Felix as a kitten, and while he had grown to be a large cat, he still had much of his playful, adolescent personality. The deli owner scratched his head affectionately.

"Hey little buddy," she said. "Are you excited about the wedding? I bet you would be, if you could understand us."

"I think he'll just be happy when I'm not so busy," Candice said, kissing the top of his head and then setting him on the floor. "I'm not getting married for another eight months. It's crazy how much there is to do."

"Trust me, I know," Moira said. "I've done it twice."

"I'm glad I have your help. Otherwise I'd be totally overwhelmed."

"I'm happy to do anything you need me to," she said. "What's on the list for today?"

"Honestly, I just want to spend a day shopping and having fun. If I see something I like for the wedding, maybe I'll buy it, but otherwise let's just relax."

"That sounds perfect to me," Moira said. "I'm just along for the ride."

Lake Marion was about the same size as Maple Creek, but was built around the lake that it was named after. It was a beautiful little town, and Moira had considered moving to it after her home of twenty years had burnt down. Fifteen minutes away from her Maple Creek — when the roads were good, at least — it wouldn't have been that far of a drive to get to work at the deli, but she had ended up moving into the little stone house halfway between the two towns instead.

Candice's Candies was right on the busiest street in town. The lower portion of the building was devoted to the storefront and the kitchen, and the upper part featured two apartments, one of which Candice had lived in for a while after first starting her business. Before its current incarnation, the candy shop had been a toy store. Moira and David had both helped with the renovations, and the deli owner felt a certain fondness for the place. Even though it was closed until that afternoon, the shop had a certain undeniable cheeriness.

"You'll have to remind me to order some more of those double filled caramel chocolates," Moira said as they passed by the candy store. "I finished the last batch just before David and I left for Europe."

"I'll try to remember to make some more for you next week," her daughter said. "They're popular. I can't keep them on the shelves."

"I'm not surprised. Have the dentists started complaining yet? You must have given half of the children in town cavities by now."

"I'm sure they're glad for the extra appointments," Candice said with a laugh. "I don't think the candy I make is any worse than what they buy in stores. It's probably healthier, since I don't use as many preservatives and I use only natural ingredients when I can."

"I'm sure it is," Moira said. "After tasting the choco-

lates you make, I don't even like store bought candy
all that much anymore."

"It's just like the difference between soup from a can
and homemade soup," her daughter said. "Homemade is always better."

"It definitely is," the deli owner said.

"Oh, has David found anyone to help him out yet?"
Candice asked. "I know someone that might want
the job if he hasn't."

"Actually... I was thinking I might do it," Moira said.
She hadn't told anyone this yet, but it felt good to
share it with her daughter. "The deli is running just
fine without me, and I need something to do with
my time. Why do you look so surprised?"

"Well, it's just that I thought you were going to try to

expand the deli? Maybe open a second location up somewhere? I know you talked about it before, and I guess I always just kind of figured that was what you were going to do."

"I do want to do that. I haven't really made up my mind yet, I guess. I need to talk to David and see what he has to say. Whatever I end up doing next, it will affect both of us."

They spent the next few hours exploring the small shops in Lake Marion. As it neared lunch time, the two of them drove to Maple Creek. They settled down in the same cafe where Moira had enjoyed coffee with her two friends the day before and shared a light lunch.

"There's something I wanted to ask you," Candice said as she picked apart her scone.

"Ask away, sweetie."

"Well, I always thought Dad would walk me down the aisle, but he's gone now, and, well... I was thinking I might ask David to do it."

Moira looked up at her daughter, surprised and touched. "I think that's a wonderful idea, Candice. I'm sure he would be delighted."

"Really? You don't think he would think it was weird?"

"Of course not. He's your stepfather. He considers you to be part of his family."

"All right, if you think he'd be okay with it... I'll ask him next time I see him."

Moira beamed at her. She loved the fact that

Candice liked David. She knew he could never replace her biological father, but hopefully he would be able to fill much of the same space he had left in her life.

The door to the cafe opened. The deli owner glanced up reflexively, then did a double take when she saw who was walking in. It was the man from the pawn shop — her top suspect in Edna's murder.

"Mom? You okay?"

She forced her attention back to her daughter and tried to smile. Her heart was beating heavily, and she kept the man in her peripheral vision. Was he going to commit another robbery right now? No, he wasn't wearing the ski mask or gloves, and there were plenty of witnesses. It didn't fit how he usually operated. *He's probably just in for a cup of coffee*, Moira thought. *Just act normal.*

That was easier said than done. She didn't want to draw any attention to herself in case he recognized her, but she also didn't want to let him out of her sight. If she tried to leave right now, Candice would surely ask why they were leaving without finishing their lunch, which would just give the man more reason to notice her. She decided to sit tight and hold her breath hoping that he wasn't going to order a meal.

She breathed a sigh of relief when he left with a coffee in hand a few minutes later. Candice kept shooting her sideways glances, but after a few minutes seemed to put it up to her mother just being weird. *That was close,* Moira thought. *Maybe David had a point. I don't want to give this guy any reason to think I'm suspicious of him. It could put not just me, but those I love in danger.*

CHAPTER TWELVE

Moira dropped Candice back off at her house a few hours later. She had enjoyed all the time spent with her daughter, but ever since running into the man from the pawn shop at the cafe, she hadn't been able to shake a clinging feeling of anxiety. She wished she had never gone to the pawn shop to see him. Putting herself at risk was one thing, but she never wanted to do anything to bring her daughter into harm's way. *David said he hasn't found anything to tie the guy to the crime yet,* she thought. *He could very well be innocent. I'm probably overreacting.*

She was still feeling uneasy as she drove back into Maple Creek. She had been planning to stop at the deli before going home to check in, but made a split-second decision as she passed the police station and ended up pulling into the parking lot. If Detective Jefferson was in, he might be able to answer a few of her questions — or at the very least, make her feel better by assuring her that the man from the pawn shop was being watched.

"Take a seat Ms. Darling." The detective stood as she seated herself in the comfortable leather chair across the desk from him, then sat down himself. "Would you like a water or a coffee?"

"I'm fine, thanks," she said.

"I know what you're here for, and I'm afraid I can't help," Detective Jefferson said. "I don't have any new information I can share with you. We did speak with one person who was linked to the robbery, but he's a minor and I'm unable to give out any names. We haven't had any real leads since."

"What about the man in the video?" she asked.

"The man in your security video?" Jefferson raised an eyebrow. "What about him?"

"Did you take him in for questioning or search his house or anything?"

"We did send an officer to speak with him and look through the merchandise in his store," the detective said. "No stolen goods were found."

"He might be a killer. Is that really all you can do?" Moira asked, feeling desperate.

"He has rights," Jefferson said. "We can only do so much without stronger evidence. From what David said, you didn't feel very certain it was him. Him being a large guy who happened to look into the camera and who owns a pair of black gloves isn't enough to grant us a warrant."

"It's hard to be certain of anything," she said. "It all happened so fast. I wish I could remember more about the man who robbed the deli. I feel like I just gave up the moment he pulled the gun."

"You didn't do anything wrong," he told her. "Memories of traumatic events often get distorted. It's perfectly normal, but it's why we can't go arresting a guy who vaguely matches the general body type of the person who assaulted you, not without more to go on."

"I understand," she said reluctantly. "I'm sorry for bothering you. It's just frustrating."

"I know it is. It's always hard when a case just doesn't move forward. Don't give up, though. We'll catch the guy responsible, eventually, if I have anything to say about it."

When Moira left the police station, she felt a little bit better. It was reassuring to be reminded that the men and women protecting Maple Creek were doing their jobs, and she was confident that eventually they would crack the case. She just wished she could be more sure about who the suspect was. The man from the pawn shop seemed to fit with what she remembered of the armed robber, but like Detective Jefferson had said, there just wasn't any concrete evidence. If she could find something tying him to the crime... *No.* She shook her head, pushing the thought away. If he *was* the killer, the last thing she wanted was for him to catch her digging around into his past. It was time to go home and let the professionals do their jobs.

Even though it was a Saturday, David was busy working. She knew that he was trying to tie up a few of his simpler cases so he could put his full focus towards figuring out who had robbed the deli and killed Edna. Moira wished that she had remembered to offer to bring him lunch while she had been in Lake Marion with Candice, but she had just been too distracted after running into the guy from the pawn shop. She would make up for it by making a nice dinner for them that evening.

She meant to start on the cooking right away, but when Maverick and Keeva greeted her at the door with their soulful chocolate eyes and happy tails, she decided that cooking could wait. It was high time that she spend some quality time with her dogs. They had been so good while she was away, and had adjusted to life with David in the house extremely well. She had no doubt that they were content, but it had been far too long since she had gone on a walk through the woods with just her and them.

Since she was already wearing boots and her coat, she just dropped her purse off inside and held the front door open for the dogs. They came dashing out and ran in a big loop through the yard. The ground was slushy with half melted snow, and muddy droplets of water flew through the air like mini missiles.

"Let's go, you two," she called. "Walk!"

She began sloshing her way across the yard to the trail head. The dogs followed behind her, pushing through the bracken and undergrowth to the sides of the trail. She knew that Keeva would need some help getting the burrs out of her fur later, but the fun that the dog was having right now made it worth it. It was easy to forget about her worries while she was surrounded by nature and had her two furry protectors close by her side.

CHAPTER THIRTEEN

Moira got to the deli on Monday in time to make the soup of the day before they began serving lunch. It was a new recipe; bean and winter squash soup. She was eager to try it, and felt sure it would go well with the gloomy winter weather they had been having.

While Darrin and Meg made crepes and prepared breakfast orders to-go for customers, she began the task of chopping up the vegetables that would be going in the soup. Garlic, carrots, onions, spinach and, of course, squash. She had a couple large butternut squashes left over in the freezer from the local farmer's market that autumn, and it was these that she had defrosted and was using now. Butternut squashes were one of her favorites, and as far as she was concerned, it was hard to go wrong with one in a soup.

Once the veggies were chopped, she dumped everything except for the spinach and the squash in a Dutch oven and began cooking them in butter. The savory scents of the cooking were beginning to fill the kitchen. She would definitely be setting some of this soup aside to take home that evening.

When the vegetables were softened, she added in chicken broth along with the squash and spices and turned the heat up until it boiled. She kept an eye on the bubbling soup as she helped her employees with the tail end of the breakfast rush. In less than half an hour, the squash was tender and ready for the next step.

Being careful not to spill any, Moira poured half of the soup into her largest blender and pureed the mixture. She added the creamy mix back into the Dutch oven and turned the burner up again, adding the beans and the spinach. The soup was all but done now, and smelled heavenly. She couldn't wait to taste it, and more importantly, couldn't wait to see what her customers thought of it.

While the soup boiled, the deli owner sat down at the counter and pulled out her tablet. It was long since time to update the deli's website. She hadn't even looked at the thing since before leaving for her honeymoon. Darrin, she knew, had been updating it with the specials, but that was about it. There was a whole page of unread emails in her inbox. About a third of them were people who were asking about her catering service. She had put the catering portion of the business on hold while she was gone, but it looked like it was time to get it up and running again.

Reading through the emails and looking at the reviews made her think again about what Candice had said when she had mentioned working as David's assistant. Did she want to open a second deli in another location? It wasn't a very simple question to answer. If she had been single, with no children, the answer would probably have been yes, but she didn't know how she could leave Candice behind and ask David to move to another town so she could start up a second deli.

We may not have to move, she thought, pondering the idea. *I could build it in another local town, or even see if Darrin would be interested in managing it.* If she did end up expanding the business, she would want to choose a location further to the south — somewhere with a higher population and more major roads going through it. A city like Traverse City might be too expensive for the time being, but if she could find a nice, smaller town on the outskirts of some place like that, she was sure she would get a lot of business.

"Hey, Ms. D, a customer is asking for soup. Are we ready to start serving lunch?"

The deli owner returned her focus to the present,

where she was supposed to be in charge of making the soup of the day. She got up and dipped a ladle into the bubbling pot. The spinach was cooked through, which meant that the soup was ready to eat.

"We're ready," she told Darrin. "Take the order, and I'll bring out a bowl. Do they want that for here or to go?"

Moira clocked out for the day after she finished helping with the lunch rush. She planned to stop by the office and bring David a to-go bag before heading home and doing some reading. It was getting easier to take a step back from the day-to-day operations of the deli, and she found it extremely rewarding to see how well it was doing without her micromanaging everything. Darrin was really shaping up to be a phenomenal manager, and all her other employees were hard-working and reliable. It had taken her a few tries, but she seemed to have finally found the perfect team.

With the doggy bag on the passenger seat, Moira pulled out of the deli's parking lot and turned towards home. She had made the drive a thousand times, and was on autopilot as she drove down Main Street. It wasn't until she was passing the last block in town that she saw them. Police cars were lined up outside of the little corner cafe that she and Candice had eaten at the day before.

CHAPTER FOURTEEN

"There was another robbery," David said over the phone. She had pulled into a gas station's parking lot to call him and ask what had happened. "No one got hurt, but he stole an expensive necklace from one of the employees."

"Oh my goodness," Moira said "David, Candice and I ate there yesterday, and the guy from the pawn shop was there. He was probably planning this while we were having lunch!"

"That was my first thought, too," the private investigator said. "I'm on my way to town now. I'll have a drive around and stop at the pawn shop while

Jefferson and his men are busy searching the immediate area around the cafe."

"Be careful," Moira said. "I hope you catch him, but I don't want you to get hurt."

"I know," he said. "I love you. I'll see you tonight."

He hung up, leaving Moira to sit in silence in the parking lot, her mind racing. She knew that she couldn't just go home while her husband was in town looking for a dangerous criminal. The waiting would drive her crazy. She decided to go back to the deli; that way, she'd be kept busy, and if something happened at least she would be close by.

"Hey, Ms. D, forget something?" Darrin asked when she walked back into the deli a few minutes later.

"There's been another robbery," she told him.

The smile fell from his face. "Where? Did he shoot someone else?"

"No, I was told no one got hurt this time," she said. "But I think I'm going to hang out here for the next couple of hours. There's a police search going on, and I want to be around in case anything happens."

"Gotcha. I hope he gets caught this time. I can't believe he's hit four different stores in just a couple of weeks."

"Me either," she said. "No one's safe."

She was suddenly struck by worry for Candice. If this guy kept holding up different shops in Maple Creek and Lake Marion, then the candy shop was bound to be on his list eventually. Eli's ice cream shop could be in danger too. *I hope David catches him red-handed,* she thought vehemently. *We've all had enough of him terrorizing us.*

The next few hours inched by until she finally got a call from David. Going into the kitchen to answer it, she crossed her fingers for good news.

"Sorry, but I've got nothing," he sighed over the phone.

"Oh." The deli owner felt a surge of disappointment. "You didn't find him?"

"I found him all right," he said. "He was sitting behind the counter of the pawn shop like nothing happened. There was no evidence that he had left the shop, and it's been open since this morning. After Jefferson finished up at the cafe, he stopped by and questioned the guy as well. I don't know if he's the one that did it, but if he did he's definitely a good liar."

"There's nothing you can do?" she asked.

"I've got one more trick up my sleeve," he said. "I'm not sure if it will pan out, but if Jefferson and I work together, I think it might."

"All right," she said. "Is there anything I can do to help?"

"I don't think so, but I'll call you if there is."

They hung up, and Moira set her phone down. She was proud of her husband; he was such a smart, driven man. She had no doubt that between him and Jefferson, they would be able to solve the case. *I really did get lucky when I met him*, she thought. She hoped that he knew how she felt. They had both been so involved in their own personal lives since they got back that it felt as if they had lost some of the closeness that they had on their trip.

"Ms. D, Meg had to clean up a spill. Can you get this order?" Darrin asked, poking his head through the door that lead to the kitchen. "We're slammed out here, I can't leave the register."

"Sure thing," she said, taking the order slip from him. She tied on an apron and washed her hands. Her husband was doing his job, and it was time for her to focus on hers.

By the time that they closed that evening, all three of them were exhausted. It had been an unusually busy day. Belatedly, Moira realized that they must have gotten a good portion of the customers that normally frequented the cafe. It had probably closed for the day after the robbery. She wasn't complaining; the extra sales were always nice. She was glad that she had decided to come back to be closer to the action. The extra business would have been a lot for her two employees to handle on their own.

"You two can get going," she said. "I'll finish up closing. I don't think we're going to get much more business in these last few minutes."

"You sure? Thanks, Ms. D," Meg said. "I'm beat. I'm glad I have tomorrow off."

"I'm opening tomorrow," Darrin groaned. "I'm going to need an extra cup of coffee in the morning."

Moira laughed and ushered the two of them out the door. "You two had better hope that cafe never closes down, or we might be this busy all the time."

Alone in the deli, she looked around fondly at the familiar walls before heading back into the kitchen to finish doing the dishes. She was still waiting on a call from David to hear whether or not whatever he and Detective Jefferson were working on panned out. She had a feeling that it would be a late night for the two of them.

She had was just about to put last plate on the drying rack when she heard the front door jingle open. Wondering which employee had forgotten something, she pushed through the swinging door to the dining area to see who it was. Her breath caught in her throat when she saw the man from the pawn shop. The plate she was holding slipped through her fingers and shattered on the floor.

CHAPTER FIFTEEN

"Are you okay?" the man asked. He began walking towards the counter. He had a limp, one that Moira hadn't noticed at the pawn shop.

"I'm fine," she muttered. She glanced down at the shards of the broken plate on the floor. She didn't want to take her eyes off the man to bend down and clean it up. "It just slipped."

"It happens. One of your employees will clean it up for you, I'm sure. The benefits of being a boss, eh?"

"How do you know I'm the boss?" she asked. She was careful not to mention that she was there alone. He might not try anything if he thought there was someone in the kitchen who would call the police.

"Your website," he said. "It's got your picture on it. I sent you an email about catering, but I haven't heard back. I'm glad to catch you here at last. I just came in for a cup of coffee and a sandwich, but if you've got time I'd like to talk to you about my daughter's party."

She looked blankly at him for a moment, trying to gather her thoughts. He wanted to talk about catering. He wasn't here to kill her. Or was he just trying to get her to let her guard down?

"Um, okay. Let me put your order in, then we can talk about catering. You'll be one of our first orders of the new year." She forced a smile and walked up to the register. "Whenever you're ready."

"Just a black coffee and whatever your sandwich of the day is," he said. "I usually grab something at the cafe on the corner on my way home, but it was closed. I like this place, though. You've got good food."

She punched the order in, hoping he didn't notice her shaking fingers. Was it just a coincidence that he had mentioned the cafe, or was he baiting her? She wondered if he realized that she had been there yesterday at the same time that he was. Was he here to tie up loose ends?

"Will that be cash or credit?" she asked.

"Cash. I think I've got exact change, hold on..." He reached into his coat pocket. As he did so, the jacket pulled away from his body enough that she could see the grip of a pistol poking out of the top of his waistband. She felt as if she had been doused in ice water.

"I'll — I'll go put the order in," she said quickly. Before he could respond, she had slipped back into the kitchen and was leaning against the swinging door. She pushed in the floor lock, but knew from experience it wasn't very sturdy. She looked around frantically for something to block it off, but there wasn't anything heavy enough in the room. Besides, the door opened both ways, so he'd be able to get in even if she had pushed a table in front of the door.

He has a gun, she thought. *That has to mean he's guilty. What do I do?* She pressed her ear against the door to see if she could hear what he was doing, but she couldn't make out any sounds. Was he still standing at the register, or was he sneaking around the counter? At any second he could throw his body against the door, and she didn't want to bet her life on the flimsy lock. She patted her pockets, trying to remember what she had done with her phone. The last time she had seen it had been when she was talking to David. Her eyes landed on the counter on the far side of the room. Sure enough, her phone was right where she had set it.

"Is everything okay in there?"

Moira cleared her throat and tried to sound convincing as she shouted back, "Fine!" She knew that she was doing a terrible job of acting normal, but at this point she had the feeling that it didn't matter.

She hurried across the room and seized her phone off the counter. Returning to her spot with her back against the swinging door, she dialed David's number from memory. It rang through to voicemail. She swore and tried again with the same result. What was going on? It had been hours since she had heard from him. Even if a murderer hadn't been waiting in the other room, she would have been worried. Last she had heard, he and Detective Jefferson had some sort of plan up their sleeves to catch the man responsible for the robberies. What if it had gone terribly wrong? What if the man from the pawn shop had done away with them both, and was now here to get her? She let out a squeak of fear as a loud knock sounded on the door to the dining area.

"I'm just going to get going," he said loudly through the door. "Sorry, but I've had a long day. I didn't know it would take this long."

She didn't reply, but kept her ear pressed to the door, listening for the jingle of the bells on the front door. When her phone rang, she nearly jumped out of her skin. The caller ID told her it was David. She let out a sigh of relief.

"Hey," he said when she answered. "We know who it is."

"I know," she whispered. "He's here. He has a gun. I need help."

"Where are you?" he asked sharply. "At the deli?"

"Yes. I'm in the kitchen. The pawn shop guy is in the front room. He said he was leaving, but I don't believe it."

"Wait, the pawn shop guy? Ewan? Moira, it's not him. It's —"

She heard a muffled swear, then a clattering sound and the line went dead. David's phone went straight to voicemail when she tried calling back. *What's going on?* she wondered. *And what does he mean that the guy from the pawn shop isn't the killer? Who else could it be?*

She didn't know the answers to any of those questions, but one thing she did know was that she trusted David. She also knew that she had just made a huge fool of herself. If the guy from the pawn shop really was innocent, then she had probably just confused the poor man half to death.

Moira shoved the cell phone into her pocket in case David called back, then steeled herself and opened the door. The dining area was empty. True to his word, the man had left. She felt a rush of embarrassment. He must think she was psychotic, the way she had acted towards him.

What about his gun, though? she wondered as she began picking up the pieces of the broken plate. She tried to think logically, like David would. *Well, he does own a pawn shop. He probably keeps it for self-defense. Plenty of people have a license to carry concealed. It's likely that he wasn't doing anything wrong at all.*

She was glad that he had gone, purely so that she could be embarrassed alone. She resolved to find his email and offer him a great deal on catering. And in the future, she needed to remember to think things through before she overreacted.

CHAPTER SIXTEEN

By the time she got the broken plate cleaned up, it was time to lock up and call it a night. She had to admit, she was going to be glad to get home and forget about this day. She flushed with embarrassment whenever she thought about how she had acted around the man from the pawn shop, and she didn't think she'd ever be able to look back on this night without turning red.

She tried calling David again as she locked the deli's front door behind her. It had only been about ten minutes since the dropped call, but that should have been plenty of time for him to get to an area with better service and call her back if the call had been dropped. She was starting to get worried, but was trying not to let herself go into full blown panic mode. At the back of her mind, images of David in a car wreck kept flashing through her mind, but she did her best to ignore them. If he didn't call her back within another ten minutes, *then* she would begin to worry.

Moira fumbled with her keys for a moment before getting her SUV unlocked. She put the to-go container of soup on the passenger seat, then walked around the back of the car to avoid the puddle of slush by the front wheels. Her nerves were already taut, so when she saw a dark shape walking down the sidewalk, she almost let out a scream. It took her a moment to recognize one of her regulars, Luis Hewitt.

"Hi, Luis," she said, relieved. "Cold night for a walk."

"Not too bad," he said. "You closing alone?"

"Yeah. I let the others go home early. It was extremely busy tonight, and I felt bad for them."

"That's nice of you," he said. "Have a good evening."

"You too, Luis," she said, giving him a quick wave.

As he passed her, his phone went off, playing the beginning notes of a song that she faintly recognized. He pulled it out of his pocket. She saw something glittering catch on the corner and fall out of his pocket. He didn't seem to notice. She hurried forward and picked it up off the ground.

"Hey, Luis, you dropped your..." She trailed off as she realized what she was holding. It was a gorgeous diamond necklace. She remembered her conversation with David earlier that day: "*No one got hurt, but he stole an expensive necklace from one of the employees.*"

When he turned and saw her holding the necklace, their eyes met for a split moment. In that moment, Moira knew that she had made a very, very bad mistake. It seemed so obvious now, looking back. Luis had been there the morning of the robbery. He had probably been checking to make sure she was back and working that day. He had also been at the cafe a few days before the most recent robbery; she remembered saying hi to him as she left with her friends. He was familiar enough with the deli that he would have been able to describe where the security cameras were, and had probably been so careful about covering his tracks because he had been afraid that she would recognize him.

"I'll take that," he said, holding out his hand. She saw his other hand move slowly towards his jacket. She was sure that he was hiding a gun underneath.

Thinking fast, Moira held out the necklace as if she was going to hand it to him. When he reached for it, she flung it as far away as she could. It landed in a pile of snow at the edge of the street. Luis's head turned automatically to follow it, and that was when Moira ran for it.

With the deli already locked up, she knew she didn't have a chance of getting inside before he caught up. Instead, she made a beeline for her vehicle. She pulled open the closest door and jumped in, slamming it shut and then hitting the lock button on her key fob. The locks clicked down reassuringly. She breathed a sigh of relief, but knew that she wasn't safe yet.

Luis pounded on the rear window hard enough to shake the whole SUV. "Come out," he yelled.

She ignored him and instead climbed onto the front seat and slid in front of the steering wheel. The engine started without fuss, but by then Luis had made it around the car and was standing by her window. His gun was pressed to the glass, and was pointing directly at her face.

"If you put it in gear, I will shoot you," he said, loudly enough that she could hear him through the window.

Moira froze. She fully expected the gun to go off at any second. She felt a pang at the thought of leaving David and Candice behind, but at least she knew her daughter was safe.

"Roll down the window," he said, motioning with the gun.

She did as he said, seeing no other option. She stopped the window halfway down.

"I don't want to hurt you," he said.

"Then just put the gun away," she begged. "I won't tell anyone."

"I don't think that's true," he sighed. "You need to convince me you won't talk. What's going to keep your tongue tied when I'm not holding a gun to your head?"

She opened her mouth, then shut it again. Her mind was completely blank. The truth was, and he knew it as well as she did, if he let her go, she *would* tell the police.

"Why did you do it?" she asked instead. "Steal from me and kill Edna? I think we both know how this is going to end, so it can't hurt to tell me."

He shifted on his feet, looking uncomfortable. "Look, I didn't mean to hurt anyone, all right? I needed the money, and my girlfriend works for a jewelry store. She told me how expensive all that stuff was — your ring, the necklace, the earrings I took from the first lady, Edna's watch... I mean, I'm going to make about ten grand in all when I sell it. Maybe a bit more if I can get good prices."

"So, you decided to become a criminal just because you could use a little bit of extra cash?" Moira asked. "How could you steal from people you know?"

"It's just stuff," he said. "I figured I needed the money more than you." He wouldn't meet her eyes. She felt some satisfaction at the thought of causing him emotional discomfort. At least if he killed her, he might feel guilty about it afterward.

"Why did you kill Edna? Even if you were desperate for money, ending someone's life is going too far."

"I know," he said, surprising her. "I didn't mean to. That... that was in self-defense. She attacked me with a bat. It wasn't murder!"

He was getting agitated, so Moira decided not to point out that the only reason Edna had attacked him was because he had been pointing a gun at her in the first place. The fact that he was getting emotional was promising. It meant that he was capable of empathy. Maybe, if she was lucky, she could play to his good side and get out of this without getting shot.

"If you shoot me right now, it will definitely be murder, plain and simple," she said. She raised her hands. "I'm not threatening you. I'm not going to attack you. I just want to go home to my family."

"Look, I said I don't want to shoot you," he said. "But I also don't want to go to jail. This has all gone too far. I just want to start over."

While he was talking, something in the rear-view mirror had caught Moira's eye. Movement. Someone was sneaking up on them. She felt a surge of hope. If she could just keep him talking a little bit longer...

"If my promise not to tell anyone about this isn't good enough, then what is?" she asked. "Just tell me what I need to do to be able to go home tonight."

"I don't know, let me think!" He kicked at her tire, his face pinched with stress. He wasn't pointing the gun at her any more, which was an improvement. It hung limply at his side. "Your daughter," he said after a moment. "You've got one, right? I think you mentioned her before. Give me her address. If you tell anyone, I'll kill her. If you keep your promise, she'll be fine."

"Not a chance," Moira said flatly.

"If you're telling the truth about keeping your mouth shut, she'll be fine," he said, sounding annoyed. "It's the only thing I can think of."

She hardly heard him. She was focused on the shape of a man coming around the corner of the deli.

Detective Jefferson. She didn't know what he was planning, but she knew she had to keep Luis's attention on her.

"I'm not going to put my daughter in danger," she said. "There must be something else. You've been coming to the deli for years, Luis. Why can't you just trust me?"

He was opening his mouth to respond when he collapsed as suddenly as if he had been shot. His body convulsed, and Moira followed two wires with her eyes back to the taser in Detective Jefferson's hands. Next to her, the passenger side door opened and a pair of familiar hands grabbed her by the shoulder and guided her out of the car. David wrapped her in a hug, and she clung onto him for dear life.

EPILOGUE

"How did you know I needed help?" she asked him. They were sitting together in the deli, which she had reopened to give them somewhere to get out of the cold while the police went over the crime scene.

"Well, some of the last words I heard from you were about a man with a gun at the deli. I figured *something* must have been going on, even though you mentioned Ewan — the man who owns the pawn shop — instead of Luis."

"He was here earlier and, well, I overreacted," she said. "What happened, why did the call drop?"

151

"I dropped my phone," he admitted, giving a dry chuckle. "I was getting in the car and it slipped out of my hand. The screen shattered, and something inside must have been damaged. I'll have to pick a new one up tomorrow."

"You told me that the pawn shop guy wasn't the killer. How did you know?"

"The kid who spray painted your cameras came clean and told us everything," he said. "At first, he denied knowing anything, but I had a feeling he was lying. This evening, Detective Jefferson and I took him to the county jail and showed him what happens to people who grow up to be on the wrong side of the law — with his mother's permission, of course. He ended up admitting that he knew the name of the guy who had hired him to black out the security cameras. That's how we knew it was Luis."

"Hopefully that kid learned his lesson," she said. "Is he going to get in trouble for what he did?"

"He'll probably get community service or probation," David told her. "We don't think he knew that Luis was planning on an armed robbery. Luckily for him, Edna didn't have any security cameras. If she had, and he had helped Luis black them out, then he might have been looking at accessory to murder right now."

"Well, I guess that's lucky for the kid," she said. "Though he sounds like he was old enough to know what he was doing was wrong anyway. What about Luis? Will he be okay?"

"He should be fine. He'll be up and about to testify at his trial."

"That's good." She shivered. "It's still so hard to believe that it was him. He has come into the deli a couple of times a week since it first opened. He seemed so normal. How could things have gone so wrong?"

"One bad decision led to another, and this is where he ended up," her husband said. "I'm just glad that he didn't hurt you."

"Me, too," she said, giving him a faint smile. "I'm definitely glad about that."

He gave her a gentle kiss, then rose from his seat. "I'm going to go see if Detective Jefferson needs anything else from us. You sit tight."

She watched him through the window as he spoke with the detective. He was her rock. It was hard to imagine where she would be right now if she had never met him. He made her life better in so many ways, and she could only hope that she did the same for him. She was sure there would be bumps in their relationship in the years to come, but she knew that when it mattered, he would do anything he could to help her or Candice — and she, of course would do the same for him. They were family, after all, and that meant they would always have each other's back.

Book34: A Saucy Taste of Murder

Book 35: A Crunchy Crust of Murder

Book 36: Shrimply Sublime Murder

Book 37: Boldly Basil Murder

Darling Deli Series

Book 1: Pastrami Murder

Book 2: Corned Beef Murder

Book 3: Cold Cut Murder

Book 4: Grilled Cheese Murder

Book 5: Chicken Pesto Murder

Book 6: Thai Coconut Murder

Book 7: Tomato Basil Murder

Book 8: Salami Murder

Book 9: Hearty Homestyle Murder

Book 10: Honey BBQ Murder

Book 11: Beef Brisket Murder

Book 12: Garden Vegetable Murder

Book 13: Spicy Lasagna Murder

Book 33: Murder, My Darling

Killer Cookie Series

Book 1: Killer Caramel Cookies

Book 2: Killer Halloween Cookies

Book 3: Killer Maple Cookies

Book 4: Crunchy Christmas Murder

Book 5: Killer Valentine Cookies

Asheville Meadows Series

Book 1: Small Town Murder

Book 2: Murder on Aisle Three

Book 3: The Heart of Murder

Book 4: Dating is Murder

Book 5: Dying to Cook

Book 6: Food, Family and Murder

Book 7: Fish, Chips and Murder

Cozy Mystery Tails of Alaska

Book 1: Mushing is Murder

AUTHOR'S NOTE

I'd love to hear your thoughts on my books, the storylines, and anything else that you'd like to comment on—reader feedback is very important to me. My contact information, along with some other helpful links, is listed on the next page. If you'd like to be on my list of "folks to contact" with updates, release and sales notifications, etc.... just shoot me an email and let me know. Thanks for reading!

Also...

... if you're looking for more great reads, Summer Prescott Books publishes several popular series by outstanding Cozy Mystery authors.

CONTACT SUMMER PRESCOTT BOOKS PUBLISHING

Twitter: @summerprescott1

Bookbub:
https://www.bookbub.com/authors/summer-prescott

Blog and Book Catalog:
http://summerprescottbooks.com

Email: summer.prescott.cozies@gmail.com

YouTube:
https://www.youtube.com/channel/UCngKNUkDd WuQ5k7-Vkfrp6A

And...be sure to check out the Summer Prescott Cozy Mysteries fan page and Summer Prescott Books Publishing Page on Facebook – let's be friends!

To download a free book, and sign up for our fun and exciting newsletter, which will give you opportunities to win prizes and swag, enter contests, and be the first to know about New Releases, click here: http://summerprescottbooks.com

Made in the USA
Las Vegas, NV
26 August 2024

94465984R00095